Noah

With love

Great Greey Rosee

RSPB

My First Book of Garden Birds

**Mike Unwin
and Sarah Whittley**

Illustrated by
Rachel Lockwood

A & C BLACK • LONDON

For Dean. *R.L.*

Original concept by Rachel Lockwood and Sarah Whittley

Reprinted 2007 (twice)
First published 2006 by A & C Black Publishers Limited
38 Soho Square, London W1D 3HB
www.acblack.com

ISBN 978-0-7136-7678-5

Editor: Clare Hibbert
Art director: Terry Woodley

Printed in China by 1010 Printing International Limited

A & C Black uses paper produced from elemental chlorine-free pulp,
harvested from managed sustainable forests.

To see our full range of books
visit **www.acblack.com**

CONTENTS

Birds in your garden

Gardens come in all shapes and sizes. Each one can be a home for birds. More birds will visit your garden if you give them what they need. Ask a grown-up for help.

All birds need food. They'll take seeds, nuts and other treats from a bird table or feeder. Water is important too, for washing and drinking. Keep a birdbath topped up all year round.

Birds need trees and bushes where they can nest. Put up a nestbox, out of reach of cats. Thistles and other weeds are good because they provide tasty seeds and insects.

Are you ready to meet some garden birds? Read the clues on each GUESS WHO? page and see if you can guess the bird. You'll find the answer on the following page.

Working it out

It can be tricky to know which bird you have seen. These questions will help you decide:

What colour is it? Can you see any special markings, such as spots or stripes?

What shape is its beak? Is it long or short, thick or thin?

What is it doing? Is it hanging from a feeder or hopping along the lawn?

GUESS WHO?

Is that a mouse scurrying about? No, it's a little brown bird with a perky tail.

What a big noise this tiny bird makes! It rattles out its song, then scoots back into the undergrowth.

But who is it?

Wren

The wren may be tiny, but it has one of the loudest voices around. Its "tick tick!" alarm call can even scare a cat.

Wrens don't often visit bird tables. Instead they creep under bushes or along walls, snapping up insects in their sharp little beaks.

GUESS WHO?

Just look at this colourful little acrobat trying to grab a peanut. Sometimes it even hangs upside down.

"Churr, churr, churr!" It's only small, but it scolds bigger birds when they try to push in.

Who is it?

9

Blue tit

A blue tit is blue, green and yellow, with a cheeky, stripy face. It's so light that it can feed from the thinnest branches, where bigger birds can't reach.

Blue tits nest in tree holes – or nestboxes, if you put them up. They love peanuts and bird cakes, and are often first on the feeders.

GUESS WHO?

This little bird is very shy. It nips in, grabs a peanut, then dashes off when the other birds arrive.

It's not as bright as a blue tit, but it's about the same size.

Who can it be?

11

Coal tit

The coal tit has a black-and-white face, and an extra stripe of white on the back of its head.

It's not as bold as other tits at feeders, but look up high in fir trees. You might see one busily searching for insects.

GUESS WHO?

What a smart-looking bird! It's blue, green and yellow like a blue tit, but it's bigger and has a black-and-white head.

It looks for food everywhere, dangling up high in the branches or hopping down on the ground. This one's visiting a bird table.

Who is it?

Great tit

A great tit is bigger than other tits. And it's the only one with a thick, black stripe down its tummy.

"Tea-cher, tea-cher!" it sings, over and over again.

The great tit loves to visit feeders. It may even take food from your hand.

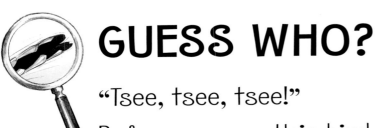

GUESS WHO?

"Tsee, tsee, tsee!"
Before you see this bird,
you might hear its
squeaky little voice.

There it is, high
in the hedgerow.
Its tummy looks
pink and fluffy,
and it has a very
long tail.

But who can it be?

15

Long-tailed tit

A long-tailed tit has a long, black-and-white tail, just like its name says. Its face is striped like a tiny badger.

These little birds stick together. Where there's one, there are probably ten.

First you hear them, then you see them – flitting from tree to tree.

GUESS WHO?

This bird likes being around gardeners. It perches on spades and snaps up insects from the ground.

From behind it looks plain brown. But when it turns around, you're in for a colourful surprise!

Who is it?

Robin

The robin has a bright red face and breast, just like on a Christmas card. It looks fatter in winter, when it fluffs itself up to keep warm.

A male sings his lovely song all year round – sometimes even at night. He's a fierce fighter, too.

GUESS WHO?

This small brown bird looks like a sparrow. But it's not so chirpy – it creeps quietly about.

Look at it flicking its wing. That's a special little dance that males perform for females.

But who can it be?

Dunnock

The dunnock is stripy brown, like a sparrow.
Now look closer: its chest is smoky grey.
Its beak is much thinner than a sparrow's,
perfect for catching insects.

Dunnocks feed on the ground. They snap up
fallen seeds at the foot of the bird table.

In spring, the male perches
high on a bush to sing his
short, squeaky song.

GUESS WHO?

Up on the roof... Down in the yard... These chirpy birds are always near a building.

They look dusty brown, like the ground where they hop. But take another look and you'll see their smart markings.

Who are they?

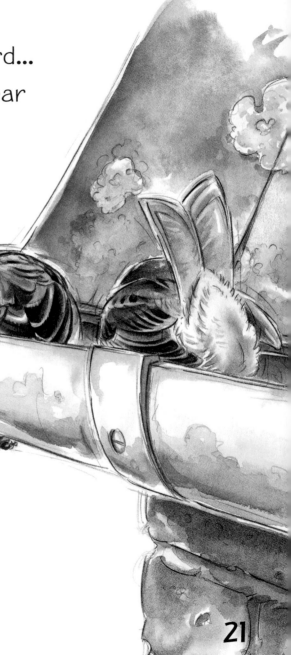

House sparrow

House sparrows live in small groups. They are noisy, cheeky and often quite tame.

You can tell a male by his grey cap, black bib and reddish-brown back. Females are streaky brown with a creamy eyebrow.

House sparrows are getting rarer. Listen out for their cheerful chirruping.

GUESS WHO?

When these birds fly past, their wings sparkle black and gold.

Look at that one, perched on a thistle. It has a bright red face – like a clown!

Such beautiful colours.

But who can it be?

Goldfinch

The goldfinch is the most colourful garden bird. It dangles from feeders and picks out seeds with its sharp beak.

Then it flutters off with a bouncy flight and a tinkling call.

Look out for big flocks in autumn. They feed near the ground – often on thistles.

GUESS WHO?

Something's peeking into its mossy nest. Look at its rosy face and blue-grey cap.

"Pink, pink!" it says, with a beakful of caterpillar. Then off it flies, with a flash of white from its wings.

Who is it?

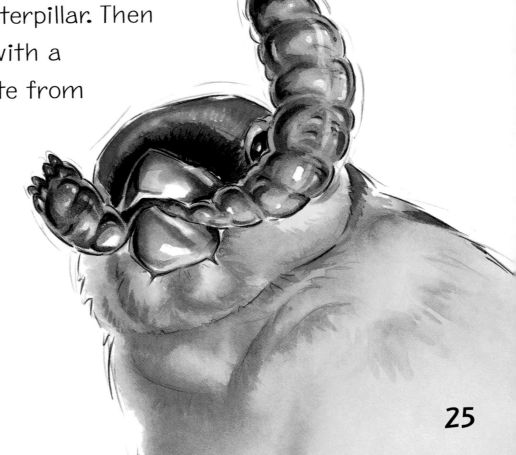

Chaffinch

The male chaffinch is very colourful. The female is plainer. She looks a bit like a sparrow, but she has white on her wings.

Chaffinches walk with little steps, like nodding clockwork toys.

They find most of their food on the ground. The adults eat seeds, but they collect caterpillars for their chicks.

GUESS WHO?

Look up! There's a bright green bird hiding in the leaves. When it flies out, you'll see the yellow on its wings and tail.

Can you see its strong, chunky beak? It uses this to crack tough seeds.

But who is it?

Greenfinch

The greenfinch is sparrow-sized, but much more colourful. Males are mostly green; females are browner. Both have yellow on their wings and tail.

In winter, greenfinches flock to feeders, where they boss the other birds around. In spring, males perch on top of fir trees to sing their wheezy, twittering song.

GUESS WHO?

Splish, splash! Some bird's taking a bath.

It soaks its feathers and scratches its head. Then it hops out and fluffs itself up to dry, wagging its long tail all the time.

But who can it be?

29

Pied wagtail

The pied wagtail is a busy little bird that never stops wagging its tail. It dashes about after insects. Sometimes it flutters up to snatch them in mid-air.

Look out for its smart black-and-white plumage. Then listen for its sharp "Chizik!" call as it flies away.

GUESS WHO?

Look at these birds, darting through the sky like arrows. They land on a wire, and then off they fly again.

Now look closer: they're black, but they're not blackbirds. Their tails are too short and their beaks too sharp.

Who are they?

Starling

Starlings are slightly smaller than blackbirds and they stand more upright.

In winter, their oily black plumage is covered in pale spots.

Flocks of starlings fuss and fight at the bird table. They make lots of different noises – some can even sound like telephones.

GUESS WHO?

"Chink, chink, chink!"

What a fuss this bird is making!

Hopping about, flicking its tail,
sounding its noisy alarm.

Its feathers are as black as night.
But its beak, when you see it,
is bright yellow.

Who can it be?

Blackbird

Only male blackbirds are black. Females and youngsters are dark brown.

You might spot one hopping across your lawn. It pauses, then – quick as a flash – pulls out a worm.

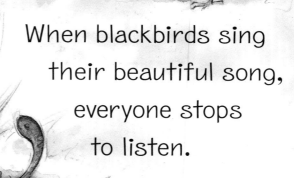

When blackbirds sing their beautiful song, everyone stops to listen.

GUESS WHO?

Watch out, snail! Here comes the champion snail-eater.

It cracks the shell on a rock – tap! tap! tap! – then gobbles up the slimy snail.

It's a brown bird with neat rows of spots on its tummy.

But who is it?

Song thrush

The song thrush is named for its beautiful voice. It makes up little tunes and repeats them over and over.

"Teedle-dee, teedle-dee, teedle-dee!" it calls. "Chip, chip, chip!"

A song thrush is usually all on its own. Look out for one hopping quietly around a lawn.

GUESS WHO?

Who's that climbing
up the tree trunk?

What a big, strong beak!
It's useful for digging
out juicy beetle grubs, or
making a hole for a nest.

**But who can this
bird be?**

Great spotted woodpecker

The great spotted woodpecker is black and white, with a splash of red under the tail. Males, like this one, have red on their head, too.

Watch one climb. It presses its tail against the trunk.

"Chick!" it calls, before flying to the next tree.

GUESS WHO?

See that black moustache and spotty forehead? This bird's looking straight at you.

But it won't stay long. Off it flies – with a splash of pink, a flash of blue.

"Screeech!"
What an ugly noise.

But who's making it?

39

Jay

Jays are tricky to watch. They fly away if you disturb them. Look out for their bright white rump as they disappear.

They are clever and crafty too. In spring, they eat other birds' eggs. In autumn, they bury acorns for a winter food supply.

GUESS WHO?

"Chaka-chaka-chaka!"

Here's a big black-and-white bird who's just landed on the road. And what a chatterbox it is.

You'll find this bird strutting along rooftops, too, trying to look important.

But who is it?

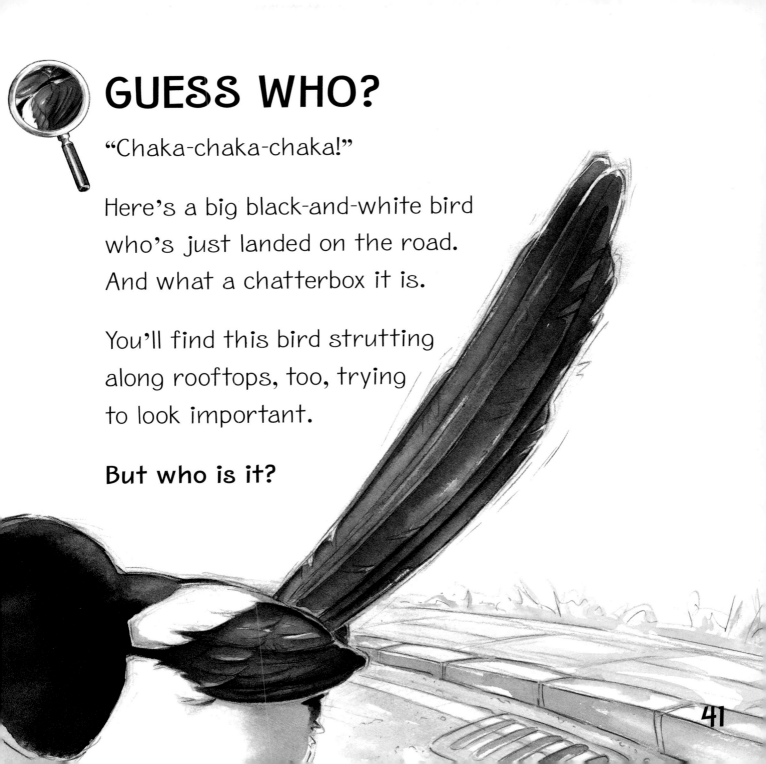

Magpie

The magpie is easy to spot. You can see its black-and-white plumage from far away.

Look closer, and you'll also see green and purple in its long, shiny tail.

Magpies eat anything – worms, kitchen scraps, even dead, smelly animals.

And they just love to scold cats.

GUESS WHO?

"Coo-COO-roo! Coo-COO-roo!"
What a lovely, gentle sound.

Can you see, up on the roof?
Two birds cuddled up side by side.

They have soft grey plumage and a
delicate black collar that
goes halfway round
their neck.

But who are they?

Collared dove

The collared dove is smaller than a woodpigeon. And it has a black mark on its neck, not a white one.

Pairs often fly around together. When they land, their tails tip up in the air.

They walk with dainty little steps, pecking up seeds beneath bird tables.

GUESS WHO?

Here's a big fat bird, hunched up and having a snooze.

When it pops up its little head, it doesn't look very clever. But look at its handsome colours: pink and grey, with a splash of white.

Who is it?

Woodpigeon

The woodpigeon is the
biggest bird in this book.
You can tell it from a collared
dove by the white on its neck
and wings.

When it takes off, its
wings make a loud,
clapping noise.

Woodpigeons waddle
along the ground looking
for seeds. And they
clamber through branches,
nibbling buds in spring or fruit in summer.

Bird words

alarm   a noise to warn of danger

bird cake food for birds, made with fat and seeds

feeder   a container of seeds or nuts for birds

grub   a young beetle

markings   the patterns on a bird's feathers

plumage   a bird's coat of feathers

rump   the part of a bird between its back and its tail

Find out more

If you have enjoyed this book and would like to
find out more about birds and other wildlife,
you might like **RSPB Wildlife Explorers**.
See **www.rspb.org.uk/youth**.

Visit **www.rspb.org.uk/youth/makeanddo/do/funbook.asp**
to download the order form and the RSPB will send you a FREE
book full of fun activities, brilliant pictures, things to make
and do, fantastic games and loads of information about birds
and other wildlife.

Who's who

Wren p7

Blue tit p9

Coal tit p11

Great tit p13

Long-tailed tit p15

Robin p17

Dunnock p19

House sparrow
p21

Goldfinch
p23

Chaffinch
p25

Greenfinch p27

Pied wagtail
p29

Starling p31

Blackbird p33

Song thrush
p35

Great spotted
woodpecker p37

Jay p39

Magpie p41

Collared dove
p43

Woodpigeon
p45